Falling For You Again!

Eugeena Patterson Family Short, #3

Tyora Moody

Tymm Publishing LLC

Falling For You Again!

A Eugeena Patterson Family Short #3

Published by:

Tymm Publishing LLC

www.tymmpublishing.com

Paperback ISBN: 978-1-961437-16-6

Eboom ISBN: 978-1-961437-15-9

Editing: Felicia Murrell

Cover Design: TywebbinCreations.com

Trust in the Lord with all your heart and lean not on your own understanding; in all your ways submit to him, and he will make your paths straight. - ***Proverbs 3:5-6 NIV***

Trust in the Lord and do good; dwell in the land and enjoy safe pasture. Take delight in the Lord, and he will give you the desires of your heart. – ***Psalm 37:3-4 NIV***

Chapter 1

I stared at the modest brick home in front of me for a long time. Afraid that a neighbor would notice me watching the house, I inhaled deeply and exhaled a shaky breath before climbing out of my Toyota Sienna.

Alright, Leesa Patterson, your mama taught you better than this.

It wasn't that I wasn't excited to pick up my kids. In fact, I missed them. No matter how exhausted my body felt, I looked forward to the hug I knew would come from my oldest and only daughter, Kisha. She always had so much to share that it was hard to keep up with the stories from her day. Knowing how my relationship changed with my mama as I got older, I didn't want this stage to end.

Then there was the burst of giggles from my son, Tyric. His laughter always tickled my ears and warmed my heart. He was a happy child, and that made me happy. My kids were growing up so fast. I truly cherished every moment.

The reality that had me in a chokehold today was I simply didn't want to face Belinda Black.

My baby's daddy's mother.

I cringed calling Chris my baby's daddy. But it was what it was. There was a time I'd thought Chris Black was the man I would settle down with for life, but that all changed not too long after our son was born. Instead, we co-parented the past two years, skirting around the tension that hung between us. And the many questions that others had for us.

What are you two? Boyfriend and girlfriend? Friends? Are you ever going to get married?

So many questions! It was easier to dodge them. Or rather, it used to be easy.

The sun beat down on my head as I walked down the driveway toward the front door. I rang the doorbell, straining to hear my children's voices. Instead, only silence greeted me, raising my anxiety. Leaving my kids with Belinda was such a different experience from when I dropped the kids off at my mama's house. It was like night versus day. I lifted my hand to ring the doorbell again, but then heard the locks disengaging from the inside.

Unconsciously, I stepped away from the door, bracing myself as the door flew open. As usual, Belinda's presence in the doorway appeared almost menacing.

Chris's dad, Emmanuel Black, passed away several years ago, but old photos confirmed Chris inherited his height from both parents. His mother stood around five feet eight or five feet nine. A salt and pepper bob framed her ebony face. With smooth skin that revealed nothing of her sixty years, she didn't wear makeup. Belinda Black was not incredibly beautiful. She was more majestic, stately... intimidating. Her wide brown eyes seemed to penetrate my soul. Never raising her voice, her words, razor-sharp, could be just as cutting. Always elegantly dressed, even though she was at home most of the day, I couldn't recall ever seeing her with her hair out of place.

With her usual scowl in place, she peered down at me through heavy brown frames perched almost on the end of her nose. A former teacher, Belinda always looked like she had a stern word to share. The last few years before retiring, Belinda served as a school principal. Every time I looked up at her, I was reminded of the times I visited the principal's office in high school and I was grateful she hadn't been my principal.

Belinda crossed her arms. "You're late again."

I bit my lip, feeling heat rise around my neck that had nothing to do with the warm June afternoon. "Sorry, I had to finish up something for my boss. If I didn't finish, I would have had to deal with it first thing Monday morning."

Belinda uncrossed her arms and placed her hands on her hips. "You could have called. If you say you are going to be here at five thirty, then I expect you to be here."

I tried my best not to grit my teeth. Sometimes it was best to not get into it with this woman. "Are Kisha and Tyric ready? I will get them out of your hair. I really appreciate you looking after them today."

Belinda seemed to be in a special mood today, so I had to ask. "Were they good?"

"They could use some more discipline."

Of course.

I fought hard not to roll my eyes. I would have preferred to leave my kids with my mama, Eugeena Patterson and her second husband, Amos Jones. My kids got along just fine with them and I didn't get these comments. But Mama and Mr. Amos had just arrived back in town last night.

The crazy thing was Belinda complained a few weeks ago about not seeing enough of the kids, mainly Tyric. Since we were taking a break from daycare for the summer months, I'd caved to Chris's request. Of course, I didn't really have a choice with Mama out of town.

"Well, come on in. No need to let my air out." The statuesque woman turned quickly on her heels, leaving me standing at the door.

I took another breath, praying I could control my emotions. *Lord, let me just gather my kids, their things and get out of here.* Mama always told me to watch my face because whatever I was feeling would be written all over it.

Chris and I grew up in similar neighborhoods in Charleston. Even though we attended rival high schools, I knew who he was. And from the Black's family home, it didn't take long to gauge that the former high school football star was his mother's pride and joy.

Chris was also her only child.

I passed dozens of familiar photos of Chris placed throughout the house on walls and surfaces. I enjoyed seeing this part of Chris's childhood and often wondered if Tyric would follow in his dad's footsteps. Tyric's baby pictures were almost a replica of Chris's photos.

We passed the living room that rarely allowed for guests. I followed Belinda past the kitchen into a family area that once had been a porch. The bright room with its large windows faced an immaculate yard filled with roses and other flowers. It was a pretty day to be outside, but Kisha and Tyric sat on the couch in front of the television. Both looked subdued. Tyric's lashes fluttered as he struggled to remain upright. He often fought naptime and appeared to be in a losing battle. I was certain he was about to succumb to the much needed slumber.

Kisha, already a shy child, seemed quieter than usual. Her sullen eyes stared at the television playing her favorite show, *Wild Kratts*. She didn't seem to be bothered that her little brother's round head leaned against her shoulder.

I swallowed back my emotions, warmed by my children's bond. Kisha was a very good older sister.

Once again, I was struck by how different my kids were with Belinda compared to my mama.

Belinda wasn't one to put a hand on a child. Chris mentioned his mother had never spanked him and that his dad did all the disciplining. But he said his mom's tone of voice was enough to put the fear of God in him. With a successful career in middle and high school education, Belinda didn't seem comfortable around young children. Even though I knew she enjoyed Tyric.

Belinda claimed she didn't mind watching both kids. But I had a sneaky feeling that Belinda didn't truly accept Kisha. Despite being Tyric's older sister, Chris wasn't her dad. She was my child. I noticed no mistreatment, but Kisha was definitely standoffish with Belinda, like she knew she needed to be wary around her.

Like mother, like daughter.

I walked into the room. Suddenly my long day at the office crept into my bones making me feel droopy too. "Hey, pumpkins. Y'all ready to go home?"

Kisha didn't notice me until I spoke. Her face brightened and my heart did a somersault as I observed joy return to my daughter's face. Kisha shook her brother awake as she slid from the couch.

"Come on, Tyric. It's time to go."

Tyric cried out a little, upset from being jostled from his impending nap.

I went over to him and picked him up. "Okay, sleepyhead. It's time to go." I tickled him until he broke out into giggles.

Kisha grabbed her book bag from the floor but stood next to me like she wasn't planning on making a move without me.

I looked over at Belinda filling the doorway. Remembering my manners, I said, "Thank you again for watching the kids today. Kisha will start summer camp next week and my mama is back in town."

Something crossed Belinda's face. "I don't mind watching Tyric. I'm sure your mama has things to do. She and her new husband probably are going to want to travel again."

I bristled at the way Belinda said *new husband*. My mama had been a widow for about five years before getting remarried. I knew from a conversation with Chris that his mother had no intentions of remarrying, even though his dad had passed almost a decade ago.

I also didn't like how she only mentioned watching Tyric. She often did that.

I plastered a smile on my face. "Well, if they decide to head out of town again, I will be in touch about your schedule."

Some emotion crossed Belinda's face I couldn't interpret. I put Tyric down and guided both children down the hallway and toward the exit.

Behind me, I heard Belinda suck in a breath. "I hope that you and Chris work things out soon."

I stopped halfway from the front door and turned around to look at Belinda. "Work things out? I think we're doing just fine."

Belinda quirked her eyebrow. "It seems like you both could do more. Give these children more stability. I don't know what's wrong with young people these days. Marriage isn't the end of the world. People just be having ..."

My eyes locked with Belinda and this time I didn't care if she saw the anger in them.

Having babies.

While she had the decency to catch herself, I still fumed at how Belinda just couldn't help herself. She just had to remind me I wasn't good enough for her son. He only dealt with me because we had a son together. That he bothered with me, a woman who already had a kid, she still couldn't process it after all these years.

I remembered how my mama reacted to both my pregnancies. I thought my mama could be so judgmental. But over the years, I'd learned to appreciate my mama because there was someone so much worse than her. No matter my mistakes, my mama never made me feel worthless. Like I was just someone taking up space in her precious son's life.

I felt a small hand wrap around mine and I looked away from Belinda to see Kisha looking up at me almost like she was pleading for us to go. I turned toward the door, determined to get out of the house and to the car.

Before we reached the door, the front door swung open, and to my surprise, Chris stepped inside. My first thought was to be annoyed that we were trapped between Chris and his meddlesome mother, but then he smiled at me.

Why did that handsome face seem to make all things right in the world?

Chapter 2

Maybe he sensed my distress, but Chris showing up out of the blue somehow didn't seem coincidental. It also didn't quite make sense for him to be here since we agreed he would drop the kids off and I would pick them up. His hours could be more unpredictable than mine.

I had expressed my concern when he suggested to not use day care. He'd convinced me that his mother was lonely, and she missed seeing the kids. I wanted to say she mainly missed Tyric, but kept that to myself.

My fury toward Chris's mom from just sixty seconds ago subsided as I watched Chris scoop up both kids in his arms. Both Kisha and Tyric had run toward Chris like they hadn't seen him in forever.

He'd come by last night and brought dinner, which I really appreciated. He always listened intently to all of Kisha's stories, something I couldn't always say I did. My little quiet one could get into an overly talkative mood and I had to zone out. I really loved how Chris was attentive to Kisha as if she was his own daughter. It meant a lot to her and me, especially since her biological father had never been in her life.

Chris recently moved up the ranks in law enforcement by moving back to Charleston. Almost a year in CMPD homicide, he was the youngest detective in the department. We'd co-parented in separate cities, about an hour and half apart, but made it work. Now that he was closer, it was so much easier.

I took a peek back to observe Belinda. She'd swapped her scowl for a broad smile. Whatever my feelings toward Belinda, she adored her son and was equally happy he'd returned to his hometown. Sometimes I wondered if her being alone also prompted him to make the move. It didn't matter, all parties benefited from Chris being around.

I cleared my throat and headed outside the door. "Okay, we need to get home so we can get dinner and baths."

Kisha pouted. "Ma, it's summer. You said I could stay up later."

"Just a little later, you still need to get your bath at the same time." I turned again. "Thank you again, Belinda."

Belinda's smile wavered, but she remained cordial looking. "I look forward to seeing the kids again."

I made note that she said kids this time.

I helped the children into their car seats, peering out the side of my eye as Chris spoke to his mom. I couldn't hear what they were saying, but I could tell Belinda wasn't happy about something and she was letting Chris know.

I also noticed his face had gone blank, giving the appearance of listening. Chris did that when he wanted to keep his emotions on lock. The one person he'd never dream of upsetting was his mother. He took whatever she said and soothed her feelings.

I walked around the car and climbed in. I knew not to just drive off, though my patience waned. I could use a nice soak in a hot bath myself. I glanced over to catch Chris sauntering toward the car, his eyes on me.

My breath caught in my throat.

Despite the heat, Chris looked cool and suave in a white button-down shirt, his blue checkered tie slightly loose. His rolled up shirt sleeves fit snug against his arms, teasing the muscular build underneath. That easy going smile, along with the twinkle in his brown eyes, had me mesmerized.

How he did that after all this time stumped me.

When we first met four years ago, I was immediately attracted to him. He wore a uniform back then. Just my luck, he'd pulled me over for speeding through a school zone. He let me off with a warning and a mad beating heart that had more to do with just seeing flashing blue lights behind me.

I couldn't stop the stupid grin I knew was on my face as he leaned over and tapped the driver's side window. I rolled down the window. "Everything okay?"

Chris glanced at the house where he grew up. His mom had closed the door, but it wouldn't surprise me if she was peeking through the curtains.

He sighed softly. “Everything is fine. Hey, I meant to ask you last night. What are your plans for the weekend? I know Eugeena and Amos are back.”

“I will probably stop by their house after church on Sunday. Mama told me her and Amos are both dragging from the trip.”

Chris quirked an eyebrow. “They had fun though?”

“Oh, yeah. You know those two. What did you have in mind for the munchkins?”

Giggles erupted from the back seat where I knew little ears were intently listening to the grown people’s conversation.

Chris winked at them, his smile wide. “I was thinking we could take a family trip to the South Carolina Aquarium tomorrow. What do you all think about that?”

Both Kisha and Tyric lost their little minds. I should have been cringing at the noise level, but Chris’s use of one particular word had me almost not hearing the kids’ enthusiastic outburst.

Family.

Neither one of us used that word often. Being a family meant we needed to consider other things. Belinda's words from only a few minutes ago came to mind.

I hope that you and Chris work things out soon.

I pushed the thought to the back of my mind as Chris's voice penetrated my ears. "Okay, y'all settle down. Let's see what your mama says."

This time, I did visibly cringe and shake my head as I met his eyes. Chris knew what he was doing. After a unit in school, where she learned about fish and underwater creatures, Kisha had been asking about going to the aquarium for weeks.

He silently stared at me. That annoying, but beautiful smile still plastered on his face.

I quirked an eyebrow at Chris, letting him know I didn't care for his tactic. He could have asked me when we were not in front of the kids. But some battles weren't worth fighting. I shrugged. "Sounds like a plan. Now I need to get the kids home."

Chris stepped back as I started the minivan's engine. "I'll call you later, so we can make plans."

As I drove off, I could see Chris getting smaller in the rearview mirror. I sighed, wishing things weren't so complicated.

I'd been the one to break up with Chris, even though I loved him. Well, I still loved him.

It was complicated.

With young children, it had been one of the hardest things I'd ever done. But my mama, my siblings and friends, and even my therapist, had encouraged me.

Insecurities had plagued me all my life. I'd always been a little on the plus side, but people said I had a pretty face. I'd also been gullible when it came to guys, thus my unexpected pregnancy at seventeen with Kisha.

Chris was one of the first men I dated as a young mom. I'd worked on myself, or so I thought. But Chris, being such a good-looking guy, set off insecurities I thought I'd buried. My final straw was realizing feelings between him and an ex-girlfriend hadn't cooled off at all.

It was for the best that we weren't a couple.

Despite the breakup, an unlikely friendship had grown between us. We made a point to be a united front for the children. But being a real couple, that ship had sailed.

Was it even possible for us to call ourselves a family?

Chapter 3

Instead of driving straight home, I went to my mama's house. It was like my brain went on autopilot.

Go see Mama! Go see Mama!

I stopped by my childhood home with more frequency than I would like to admit. There was a time in my life I avoided Eugeena Patterson. We didn't get along, especially during my teenage years. My older brothers were much older than me. I know Mama tried really hard when I came along, but she was almost forty with two teenage boys and she'd been teaching hormonal eighth grade students for fifteen years. She was tired, and I got away with a lot being the only girl.

Over the years, either Mama had mellowed or maybe I had. I would have to say, at some point, Mama and

I crossed over into a friendship between two women. She was still Mama, but I relied on her wisdom more than I did when I was younger. So, I'd like to think I had matured.

She was a different person to me now, even more so since marrying Amos Jones. I was grateful Mama and Amos finally went on their long-awaited honeymoon. But I was also happy they'd return. They were gone longer than the two weeks planned and I knew they had to be exhausted, but I couldn't head home yet with my thoughts focused on Chris.

Before I turned the ignition off good, both kids were squirming in their car seats. I couldn't get them unfastened quick enough before they went running toward my mama who'd rose from her rocking chair on her front porch.

"Well, isn't this a nice surprise? There go my babies." Eugeena held her arms open wide as Kisha barreled into her arms.

Kisha yelled, "Grandma, we missed you! Did you bring us anything?"

It struck me how much my kids came out of their shell around Mama versus Chris's mama. I cleared my throat. "Kisha, don't be rude."

Mama grabbed Kisha and Tyric's hands and turned towards the front door.. "It's fine. I got something for everyone. Y'all come inside. Amos is out back with Porgy."

Porgy was a Corgi that my mom gained after a friend died a few years ago. Growing up, we didn't have pets in the house, but a lot had changed with my mama since she retired. We'd babysat Porgy, and both kids wanted to keep him, but I was more than happy to drop him off at his permanent home this morning.

Once inside the home that I grew up in, I could feel some of my worries of the day melting away. Kind of similar to Belinda's home, my mama also kept family photos in the hallway. There were many. I hadn't realized she had rearranged the photos. In the center now was a large wedding portrait of her and Amos. Mama's relationship with Amos was so different from when she was with my daddy. I was a daddy's girl, but I'd always sensed my parents didn't quite get along, even though they never really argued in front of us.

I glanced up and saw a photo of my dad. His bright smile warmed my heart and made me a little sad. I had a similar photo of him at home dressed in his doctor's coat. My dad was an obstetrician, and most of the time, during my childhood, it felt like he was delivering babies more than he was home. But when he was at home, being the only girl and his baby, Ralph Patterson made me feel special. I took his death hard and I knew being alone rocked Mama's world. With my two brothers and I out of the house, the empty nest turned really empty for her. Though she would never admit it.

It's probably why over the past few years she'd picked up a very unusual hobby since retirement. We were all glad she married her next-door neighbor, a former homicide detective. Amos was a pretty cool dude and he not only made Mama happy, he kept her in check.

I marveled at the gallery of photos until something occurred to me. Mama had added a wedding portrait of my favorite brother, Cedric, with his wife, Carmen next to my oldest brother, Ralph Jr.'s wedding portrait with his wife Janet. Everyone in the family had wedding pictures except me. I wasn't sure why that struck me so hard, but I turned away from the wall, remembering why I showed up here.

I entered the kitchen which smelled like a fresh lemon pound cake. My eyes fell on the table where one of three loaves sat. Mama had cut a few slices and was transferring them to desert plates.

I raised my eye. "Mama, we haven't eaten dinner yet."

Mama waved her hand at me. "Just a little snack. If you want something, Amos got us a family meal from the Chicken Shack. It's more than enough. We have mac and cheese and green beans for the sides."

My stomach started rumbling, but I didn't want to overstep. "Sorry to drop in without notice. If you are sure, it has been a long day."

"Girl, sit down and rest your feet. I will get y'all some plates."

Amos came in the back door with Porgy. Chaos ensued for the next few minutes as my kids insisted on greeting their canine uncle.

"Good to see you, Leesa."

"You too, Amos. I'm so glad you are both home."

Amos winked. "No place like home. Your mama told you we have plenty of food. I hadn't been to the Chicken Shack in a few weeks, and I believe they sneaked in more food than I paid for."

"Well, you are a regular." Mama clapped her hands. "Okay, you all. Kids, wash your hands so you can eat. Porgy, behave."

I shook my head. Porgy might have been a dog, but he was treated like one of the kids.

A few minutes later, my munchkins were happily licking their fingers as they demolished chicken wings. I'd eaten a plate of food and though it was good, I still felt a desire to spill my thoughts. "Mama, you cooked these pound cakes today?"

Mama grinned. "After I got our luggage unpacked and everything laundered, something about being back in my kitchen helped me settle in more. You know this is my place to be. That was the longest trip I've had away from home."

I nodded. Mama was always here. That's something we could always count on.

"I have some things for you and the kids. You want to come upstairs and get them?"

Mama had given me the eye, probably sensing my need to talk.

I followed her up the stairs and passed what used to be my childhood room. Mama had turned it into a guest room. When the kids or any family spent the night, they used my old room.

Before I stepped into her and Amos's room, Mama asked, "What's going on with you?"

I shrugged. "Just a bit down. Probably because I was over at Belinda's house."

Mama cocked an eyebrow. "Why were you at Chris's mama's house?"

"She watched the kids today. You know, this time of year when school gets out, I try to take a break from day-care. Kisha has summer camp over the next few weeks and Belinda likes to keep Tyric when she can."

Mama looked at me, but all she said was, "Mmmm."

I sighed. "She treats Kisha okay, but I know Kisha doesn't care to go over there near as much as she enjoys being with her grandma Eugeena and grandpa Amos."

"Well, of course." Mama smiled, but then she turned serious. "Did Belinda say something to you?"

Sometimes, I think one reason I backed off from Mama is because she could read me. That's what mothers do. I did that now with my two. I understood them. I knew what they were thinking sometimes before they were thinking. "Why are you trying to read my mind, Mama?"

"Because you're not saying what's going on."

"It's just that Belinda can be vocal. She would prefer Chris and I were married or probably if I would just move on. I don't think she considers me a good choice for him."

Mama huffed. "Belinda probably doesn't like anyone. I remember her when I used to work in the school system. She had a reputation of being hard, not only on her students but also on her staff. She just has one of those personalities that's stiff and unyielding. In fact, I would say the only time I've seen any softness in that woman is when she's around her son."

"Oh, yeah. Chris is her only child, and she is like a mama bear, even though he's practically thirty years old."

Mama smiled. "She's always going to be his mother. You will experience this the older Kisha and Tyric get. When other people come into their lives, you will be on alert."

"I guess. I just wished she'd keep her opinions to herself."

"Have you and Chris talked about it?"

I bristled. "About what?"

"Marriage. You spend a lot of time with each other. I can tell you both care for each other a great deal, and it's more than about being there for the kids. You may not like Belinda being meddlesome, but she has a point. Kisha is really attached to Chris."

"I know. Chris has been in her life since she was four years old. We're having *family time* tomorrow at the South Carolina Aquarium."

"That's a good thing."

"Is it?" I flung my arms out. "I mean for the kids. But we're not a family. I don't know what Chris and I are anymore."

Mama sat on her bed. "You're going to have me sounding like a broken record. Have you talked about any of your feelings with Chris?"

"No. I broke up with him. What would it look like if I'm changing my mind now?"

Mama patted the bed. "Sit down, Leesa."

I sat like a dutiful daughter.

"You never said why you broke up with Chris. I know you had postpartum depression after delivering Tyric, but it was more than that. Now I'm not trying to pry because you and me know I've been trying to do better, but you and Chris were having problems for a while."

I crossed my arms like the defiant girl I once was, but I needed to tell my truth. "Before Chris started dating me, he had a girlfriend. Isis Malone. She's beautiful. Everything I wish I was, I guess. When Chris and I started dating, she was everywhere. We couldn't avoid her."

Mama frowned. "Was she stalking Chris?"

"I don't know what you call it, but she didn't want to let him go. One night, this was a few days before I went into labor with Tyric, a few friends at work took me out for a baby shower dinner. I saw Chris with *her*. We argued that night and he said he was trying to tell her to stay away. But it looked like more than that to me. She was so close to him and he wasn't pushing her back. They were out in public where anyone could see them."

Mama had placed her hand over her chest. "Oh, my."

"After I had Tyric, it was too much. It was enough to take care of him and Kisha. Finally, I just told Chris I wanted to be near my family again. That's when I moved back down here to Charleston. I was tired of always feeling insecure about Chris. He acted like he moved on, but I got the sense that he really didn't want to push Isis away either. After I moved down here, I heard they tried to date again, but Chris broke it off again."

"Wow, sounds like Chris brought some baggage into the relationship."

"Yeah, and I had to get pregnant again. You know I didn't even know I was pregnant with Kisha when I was in high school. I sprung her on you and Dad. When I found out I was pregnant again, I barely wanted to face you. And you know what? I dreaded telling Chris. But he took it better than I thought he would."

"That's a good thing." Mama peered at me. "You have feelings for him. Do you want more?"

I blurted. "I want what you, Junior and Cedric have. I want to be married too."

There, I said it.

My mama took a breath. "I like Chris. When I first met him, I wasn't too sure about him. I get the sense over the years, like you, like all of us, he has changed and matured. That's not to say you should get married. You should only get married if you feel God says he's the one for you."

"I thought he was the one for me at one time. Chris is a gorgeous man. I mean, when we're out in public, women are always staring at him. And look at me."

"What about you? You are a beautiful young woman."

I looked at my mom. "I'm not the type of girl that Chris usually dated."

"Well, there's something about you he loves that makes him stick around. And this Isis woman, it never worked out between them. She's in his past."

I paused, thinking about what Mama was saying.

Mama grabbed my hand, startling me. "I've seen how that man looks at you. Now I know you have some insecurities, but you need to have more confidence in who you are. You've grown a lot, Leesa. Your daddy would be so proud of you. I'm proud of you. I need you to be proud of you, too. You're a single mom to two kids, and you have done a really good job. Chris moved here to be with you all. He's rose in the ranks at the CPMD. What is it I always tell you?

I repeated it. "Trust in the Lord ... and He will give you the desires of your heart." Though I knew the words, I didn't always let them penetrate my heart.

"Talk to Chris. The best way to see if this lifelong commitment is for both of you is if you learn to communicate your feelings. Don't keep them bottled up. A lifelong partner should be your dearest friend, someone you can share everything with."

Emotions rose in me, making tears sting my eyes. "I want that."

"The lifelong commitment? Because marriage is more than standing at the altar. Don't feel pressed to have the ceremony or the status of being married. Take your time and talk to him."

I smiled. "Thank you, Mama. I knew there was some reason I needed to talk to you."

She reached over and hugged me. I hugged her back, feeling like a little girl again as she rubbed my back.

Chapter 4

My eyes followed Chris as he assisted Tyric with his French fries. I had to stifle a laugh as Chris ate almost as many fries as he made sure Tyric consumed. The perks of parenting included having the occasional opportunity to have a snack during your child's mealtime. Much more independent, Kisha dipped her own fries into ketchup and turned her head from side to side while taking in all the hustle and bustle going on around us.

We had explored every corner of the South Carolina Aquarium with the touch pool being a favorite. Both kids, though timid at first, eventually touched a hermit crab, a sea urchin and a stingray. Even I touched the stingray, which drew a grin from Chris. He knew I wasn't a fan of touching anything that wasn't furry.

Our server came by. "How's it going, folks? Do you need anything else?"

I shook my head. "No, we're fine."

She smiled at us. "You have a beautiful family."

There was that word again, *family*. Chris and I locked eyes. I didn't know why I squirmed under his gaze or why the word family triggered such emotions in me. We were co-parents, but nothing would come between Chris and I.

As if sensing the shift in our dynamic, the server raised an eyebrow, her eyes glinting with curiosity. "You two certainly make a handsome couple," she remarked. A hint of mischief danced in her voice.

I froze, unsure of how to respond. Was it that obvious we weren't married? Maybe I was being super sensitive. I hoped Chris hadn't noticed how the server's comments flustered me.

Before either of us could say anything, the server cleared our empty plates off the table. I watched Chris as he wrestled with Tyric. He was such a good-looking man. I looked around to see if anyone was watching us.

Bad habit of mine.

But I always found some woman admiring Chris, even when he was holding his son in his arms and Kisha pranced alongside him. He was just one of those guys who grabbed other women's attention. Or, I could just be that insecure. I'd lost weight since having Tyric. I probably was the smallest I'd ever been and I'd always been a full-figured girl. For the first time, I fit into a size fourteen pants. I didn't enjoy going to the gym, but I had taken on monthly payments to purchase a Peloton bike. I had to keep the kids off it, but at night the bike did wonders for relieving stress.

Chris even noticed my clothes fit different. It could have been my imagination but he complimented more on my appearance lately.

As we finished our snack, I suggested we head to the sea turtle exhibit before we leave. Kisha's eyes lit up with excitement, making me smile. She had become quite the fan of sea turtles since learning about them in school.

Tyric seemed to have grown tired. Seeing that his little legs were dragging, Chris lifted him up on his shoulders.

We said little as Chris drove us back to the house. He picked up Kisha who'd fallen asleep during the ride over. Though it was early evening, I was grateful to get both kids in the bed. They would sleep well tonight.

After the sleepy duo had baths and were tucked away in their rooms, Chris joined me in the living room. I'd taken my shoes off and stretched my feet out, tired from all the walking earlier.

Chris plopped down on the other side of the couch as though he lived there. Before I could stop him, he grabbed one of my feet and started massaging it.

"You don't have to do that." I sputtered, though his touch certainly felt delightful.

He smiled. "You deserve to relax. I know being out in the crowds today was a lot on you, too."

Chris knew I wasn't the outgoing type. I tried to be, but the introvert in me drained easily around crowds. "As long as the kids enjoyed themselves, that's what matters." I barely heard what I said and struggled with wanting to pull my foot out of Chris's grasp or just letting him continue to massage it.

It felt so good.

I sighed as the warmth of his hand gently touching my foot relaxed me. I realized after a few minutes it had grown too quiet. I looked at Chris, he was staring back at me. It could have been my imagination but, for a second, he looked shy. I found it endearing because Chris wasn't a shy man. He usually said what he had to say.

This scene had become too intimate, so I pulled my foot from his grasp. "Is there something on your mind?"

He looked at the foot I pulled away but didn't touch it again. I hoped I hadn't inadvertently opened a door. Chris never spent the night.

Chris took a deep breath. "I've been thinking about something. Do you ever think about us?"

I immediately missed the warmth of his touch on my feet and pulled the blanket down from the back of the couch, covering them like I'd been naked or something. The way my heart raced as I met his gaze, I might as well have been. "What do you mean?"

"I mean, do you ever wonder if we could be more than just co-parents? If we could be a family?"

I felt my cheeks flush as I tried to find the right words. "I don't know, Chris. Is this you suggesting this or your mother?"

He frowned. "Look, I know my mom probably said something she shouldn't have, but it's me asking the question."

"What about dating other people?"

"I don't want anyone else." His voice was full of sincerity.

I was stunned, not sure what to say.

He held up his hand. "We can start slow. I was thinking it would be nice if we went out to dinner, just the two of us. No kids. What do you say?"

"You're asking me out on a date?"

He held up three fingers and grinned. "Actually, three dates."

I choked with laughter. "Three dates?"

"Yeah, I figured by a third date we both would know where to go next with our relationship."

I raised an eyebrow. "You have really thought about this."

He grinned, "I have." His smiled dropped. "Look, I know I messed up before. It's been a long time. You've seen that I've changed. I moved here not just to be closer to the kids, but to be closer to you, too."

My heart leapt in my chest. He'd never said this before. Still, I could see Belinda's face. I knew he said his mom didn't put him up to this, but it was only yesterday she had been complaining.

"Look, I feel like we both still have feelings for each other. If I'm wrong, just tell me no."

That's exactly what I wanted to blurt out, but I didn't. I was really thinking about this. But I didn't want my heart broken again.

Finally, I said, "Can you let me think about it overnight?"

He smiled. "I'm happy that you are at least going to give it some thought." He stood from the couch. "I need to head out. I'm going to church with Mom in the morning. You know she likes the early service."

I walked him to the door, my head spinning with his proposition. He turned and looked at me. "Sleep tight, Leesa."

I bit my lip. "Good night, Chris."

After I closed the door behind him, I leaned against it feeling my knees shake from more than the exhaustion of the day's activities.

Could we date each other again? Should I do this?

Chapter 5

Chris's proposition echoed in my mind all night. When I drifted off to sleep, a familiar dream visited me. The one where I walked down the aisle of Missionary Baptist Church. On both sides of the church were people I'd grown up seeing all my life. My family sat in the front with Mama smiling harder than I'd ever seen. When I turned to face the groom, I almost stumbled in confusion. I recognized the figure from the back, but why wasn't he watching me walk down the aisle toward him? Wasn't the groom supposed to be looking at his bride?

That dream lingered long after the alarm on my phone blasted in my ears. So deep in thought, I didn't notice Kisha had dressed herself in two different shoes for church service.

When we arrived for Sunday dinner, the first thing Mama said to Kisha. "Girl, I see you have matching colors, but those shoes look really different."

Kisha giggled, looking cute as she could be as I stared, horrified.

"How did we do that?" I blamed my distraction on a lack of sleep. At least that's what I told Mama.

Eugeena Patterson was a sharp one and I could tell she wanted to ask me what else was going on, but she didn't. She shook her head. "It's okay. They always say come as you are. Just as long as you came and had some spiritual feeding this morning."

I cringed on the inside because my mind had been a million miles away. It was a good thing Chris went to church with his mother this morning. I grew up Baptist, and Chris attended the African Methodist Episcopal church. I attended church service with him on several occasions and while the services were a little quieter, there was good hand clapping gospel music. And their minister preached just as hard as Pastor Jones to me.

Yeah, I was pretty sure if Chris sat next to me today, I wouldn't have gotten as much of the sermon as I did. I would have spent the whole time eyeing him, which is often exactly what happened. When Chris wasn't pre-occupied keeping the kids quiet, I would catch his eye and the curve of his smile would have me feeling some kind of way in that church pew.

Lord, forgive me!

As the kids ran upstairs to change into clothes that we kept over at Mama's house, I wandered into the hallway again, looking at the portraits on the wall. I sighed. A part of me wanted nothing more than to say yes to Chris's proposition to date again, but the scars from our breakup were still raw. *But what could it hurt?* I thought to myself.

It could hurt a lot to try this relationship thing again if it failed.

With God, all things are possible.

Well, maybe I recalled more than I thought from to-day's sermon.

Mama came up behind me. "You doing okay today? How are things going after our conversation the other day?"

"It's fine." I didn't want to tell Mama yet about the conversation I had last night with Chris. I needed someone else to talk to this time, someone more my age who understood heartbreak and love. I knew just the person, but it would have to wait until tomorrow.

Most days, I brought my lunch to work. Today, I took advantage of my hour and left the office for a change. In about six minutes, I arrived at Sugar Creek Cafe, a cute coffeeshop that also offered gourmet sandwiches and baked goods. One of the baristas had become one of my dear friends over the past few years. We bonded immediately through our mutual acquaintance, my sister-in-law and her best friend, Carmen Patterson. Both of us were single gals who'd often talked about the day we would walk down the aisle like Carmen did with my brother.

I walked through the door and the aroma of fresh coffee and baked goods enveloped me. Behind the counter,

Joss glanced up from the register and broke into a warm smile. "Hey, girl, what a nice surprise!"

Joss' gorgeous curls were pulled back in an afro puff above her head. Her pretty, bright caramel skin always had a smile.

"Hey to you too! Are you really busy right now? I was hoping we could talk."

Joss leaned over the countertop. "Absolutely. I know you have to be on your lunch break. What would you like and I will deliver it to you," she winked.

I returned the smile as some of the tension eased from my shoulders. I knew Joss had a cool boss, who also was one of my mom's former students. Whenever Mama visited the cafe, she liked to say Fay Everett had been one of her favorite students. "I will have a chicken salad croissant, an iced mocha coffee and water."

"Coming right up."

I paid for my lunch and headed toward the back. All the nooks and cozy spots was one reason I wanted to come to the cafe. There were booths near the windows, but in the back were couches and big comfortable chairs that a person could curl up in. While there was a bit of a crowd in the main dining area part, the back was really quiet. I grabbed a booth in the back corner and sank into the cushioned seat with a sigh.

A few minutes later, Joss slid my tray with my lunch in front of me. She quickly sat down. "I can tell something's bothering you, but please eat."

I took a bite of the chicken salad, savoring the buttery goodness of the croissant. "Chris wants to date again," I said quietly.

Joss's eyes widened. "Wow! How do you feel about it?"

I chewed and swallowed before responding. "That's the problem. I don't know how I feel. I told you our history and why I broke up with him. I just don't know if we are really right for each other. Yes, I know we have a son together."

"And Chris is so good with Kisha." Joss added.

I nodded. "Yeah, I really don't want to let the kids down either. I mean, what if we try again with this whole relationship thing. Trying to be serious and then it falls apart again. I don't know if I can pick back up with us being cool as co-parents. It took some time for me to work through even trusting myself around him again."

Joss nodded. "You have settled in your mind that you are both together for the kids' sake and nothing more."

"That's been a big deal the past few years."

Joss leaned over. "I know how much Chris hurt you before. But people change, and it sounds like he's trying to make things right. What exactly is he suggesting?"

I took a sip of the iced coffee, relishing the flavor. "He suggested we go on three dates. If we make it to the third date, then we can decide where to go with our relationship from there."

Joss grinned. "I say go for it."

I blinked. "You really think I should give him another chance?"

"I think you should follow your heart," Joss said gently. "I believe you two have been able to make the co-parenting work because you both still love each other. He respects you as the mother of his child. But I, and everyone else, see the way Chris looks at you. And I know you be sneaking some peeks too."

I about choked on the rest of my sandwich. "Girl, I knew you were the one to come talk to. I was hoping I wasn't being that obvious."

"Hey, it's okay. The dating idea could work. I think you are going to have to trust the process. You know what our mamas would say."

We both said it together.

"Pray on it."

"Thanks. I need to be heading out so I can walk back to work."

The rest of the afternoon zoomed by and I felt buzzed, like I was getting ready for the first day of school or something. Chris and I spending time together without the kids had been non-existent for several years, like before Tyric was born. This was a big step.

I picked the kids up from my mama's house. My mama believed in naps, so by the time I had both kids in the car, I was grateful that they both had just awakened from a nap. Kisha lacked her usual chattiness and Tyric wasn't as fussy. These were all good signs to me.

Once the kids settled down after their baths, I called Chris. "Hey, it's me."

"Hey, Leesa." The warmth in his voice made me smile. "What's up? I've been waiting to hear from you."

I took a deep breath. "I've decided… that I'd like to try going on those dates. It sounds like a good way to take things slow and see where they lead."

There was a brief silence before Chris responded. "Really? You mean it?"

"Yes," I said softly. "I mean it."

Chris exclaimed. "Thank you for giving me another chance. I won't let you down this time, I promise."

"I know you won't." And to my surprise, I believed him.

"So, dinner this weekend?" Chris asked, a hint of laughter in his tone.

I giggled. "I'd like that."

"Great, I'll pick you up at seven on Saturday."

"I look forward to it," I said and meant every word.

Chapter 6

"Leesa! Chris is here!" Joss called out from the front door.

"Okay, I'll be right there." I smoothed my hands over the fabric of my new sundress. I caught it on sale online and wasn't sure how it would fit. The buttery yellow made my milk chocolate skin pop a little extra. I didn't have time for a pedicure, so I painted my own toes with some glistening gold polish. I took one last glance at myself in the mirror, lifting one of my legs. My wedge sandals were too cute. I hoped I hadn't overdressed for the occasion, but I felt good.

I took my time walking to the living room. I rarely had a chance to make an entrance. The kids had assembled around Chris as usual, making sure they had his attention while they shared about their day's events.

Chris looked up as I stepped into the open living room. Joss grinned at me from the kitchen area. Both kids swung around too. All eyes were wide and on me.

"Wow, you look amazing." Chris's eyes moved slowly up and down my body. I couldn't recall the last time he looked at me like that.

"You look beautiful, Mama." Kisha's eyes sparkled with joy and awe.

"Thank you." My cheeks had grown warm with all the attention. Probably because I couldn't stop grinning. My cheeks must have looked like a chipmunk.

Chris wasn't looking too bad himself. Dressed in a crisp white button-down shirt and navy blue slacks, my already fraught nerves edged up a notch.

"Okay, kiddos, let your parents head out. We got popcorn to get popping." Joss had volunteered to babysit the kids, which I appreciated so much. I looked over at her and she snuck a wink in my direction. She had a few Disney movies lined up, including Kisha's favorite, the live version of *The Little Mermaid* with Halle Bailey.

Both kids gave us hugs before following Joss into the kitchen to get snacks ready for movie night. Somehow, their affections helped ease my nervousness. It was good for both of them to see Chris and I going out together.

After Joss shuffled the kids out of the living room, Chris asked. “Are you ready?”

I smiled. “Absolutely. I’m looking forward to this. Although it would be nice to know where we are going.”

Chris raised an eyebrow. “Don’t worry. You will love this surprise.”

While I’d been known to pull off quite a few surprises, I wasn’t a fan of not knowing. As I shut and locked the front door behind us, I cringed inside remembering that I’d actually said I was looking forward to the date out loud. But was that really a bad thing? I wanted Chris to know my thoughts, and I wanted nothing to mess up tonight.

Chris opened the car door for me. As I waited for him to come around the side of the car, I used my hand to smooth the tendrils I’d left hanging on the sides. I managed, with Joss’s help, to pin my shoulder length hair up in a fancy updo, not my usual hairstyle. I figured the ponytail wouldn't do, and Chris saw me wearing that style all the time.

Chris slid into the driver's seat, glancing at me sideways. "That dress is really gorgeous on you."

"I'm glad you like it."

"Oh, I more than like it," Chris chuckled.

The warmth stretched from my cheeks down my neck. I liked the way the dress tucked in, accentuating my waist, and then flared out not highlighting my wide hips.

It was the perfect dress for a date.

Chris started the car and began driving down the road, and I felt a surge of anticipation for the evening ahead. I couldn't help but miss the chatter of the children in the backseat. Their absence left an unfamiliar silence between Chris and me as he drove us to our destination. He wouldn't tell me where we were going, but I trusted him to pick a great place for dining.

I gasped when the restaurant came into view. Fleet Landing was an elegant restaurant, which used to be a place for sailors back in World War II. I knew reservations were required to dine inside the place. I'd never eaten there before, but Mama and Amos had been a few times.

"Here we are," Chris announced as he parked the car. "I thought you might like this place."

I gazed at the twinkling lights reflecting off the water and felt a flutter of excitement. "It's beautiful."

Once inside, a breathtaking view of the Atlantic Ocean greeted us at our table. The sunset painted the sky in hues of pink and orange, casting a warm glow over everything. I took a deep breath, inhaling the salty scent of the sea air mixed with the aroma of delicious food. I was enjoying the scenery so much I forgot to look at the menu.

A server showed up at our table. "Have you decided what you'd like?"

"Oh, yeah." After quickly browsing and noticing how high the prices were, I decided. "I think I'll go with the Charleston Shrimp and Grits."

"I'll have the Chargrilled New York Strip with Seared Shrimp," Chris added, closing his menu.

As we waited for our meals, the conversation naturally flowed to our day at work. My job wasn't as interesting as Chris's, and definitely less stressful. A few years ago, I got a job as an administrative assistant at an insurance company. My boss encouraged me to take classes and last year, I officially became an insurance adjuster. The increase in pay and the challenge of the job was what I needed, but sometimes it was stressful dealing with clients and their claims.

Being the son of a cop, Chris always knew he wanted to be in law enforcement. When we first met, he was still in uniform but talked often about becoming a detective. Still a rookie, he'd been on the Charleston Police Department homicide team for almost a year. He didn't always talk about his cases, even though some of them ended up on the news. But I always tried to keep our conversations light and encouraging, focused on the kids.

We ate in a comfortable silence, enjoying the meal and the view. While leaving the restaurant, Chris grabbed my hand. This surprised me, but I didn't pull away. It felt nice walking hand-in-hand, back toward the car. The ride back to the house wasn't as awkward as before. In fact, it felt comfortable and full of promise.

After Chris pulled the car into the driveway, he cut the engine.

"Thank you for tonight, Chris. You want to come in and say good night to the munchkins?"

"Of course."

Joss, Kisha and Tyric were all knocked out on the couch and sleepily greeted us as they tried to shake their grogginess. Chris took both kids to their rooms.

"Were the kids good?" I asked Joss as she grabbed bowls and headed to the kitchen.

"We had a blast. Thanks for letting me spend time with them. How did the first date go?"

I grinned and clasped my hands together. If I could have floated off the floor, I would have.

Joss giggled. "By the look on your face, it must have been one awesome date. Let me get out your hair. I will want all the details tomorrow."

After Joss left, I slipped out of the wedge heels and grabbed two bottles of water from the fridge. Chris came into the kitchen and I handed him a bottle of water.

I inquired. "Everyone down for the night?"

Chris took a swig of water before replying. "Oh, yeah. They were both so tired. From what Kisha tried to tell me, it sounds like they had a good time. Speaking of good time…" Chris held his hands up. "So, not bad for the first date."

"No, you didn't do too bad. You still have two more dates to go."

"I got this. No problem." He walked over to me and took my hand. "I should really get going, but I have to do this first."

Before I could say anything, Chris pulled me in close and kissed me. His lips were soft against mine and unlocked memories I'd stored away. The kiss lasted a few moments before we slowly parted. He brushed his fingertips against my cheek.

"Sleep tight, Leesa."

I followed him to the door in a daze.

That kiss!

Chris lingered at the door for a moment, sparks of electricity running between us.

I swallowed. "Good night, Chris."

He nodded and opened the door.

When I closed the door, warmth radiated my body as it buzzed with emotions.

I stumbled off to bed feeling completely overwhelmed and also appalled with how close I was to asking Chris to stay the night.

Chapter 7

One week had passed since the first date, and for the past seven days, I'd floated on the possibilities that lay ahead for the future. Chris and I could make this work this time. I wasn't sure why one dinner date had me feeling head over heels in love.

I imagined some of it had to do with that unexpected kiss and the flood of emotions that I couldn't seem to stop.

It's what I'd wanted for so long.

Tonight, I'd dropped the kids off with Mama and Amos. I told Chris he could pick me up at Mama's house. I peeked out the living room window waiting for Chris to pull up. My heart fluttered with anticipation as I rubbed my hands on my sundress.

It wasn't as bold as the dress I wore last week, but the pastel pink made me feel pretty. The puffy sleeves felt comfortable and I liked the snug fit. The only problem was the neckline, which plunged lower than I'd expected.

Behind me, Mama appeared with something shiny in her hands. When I finally told her about Chris's proposition and the three dates, you'd thought I'd won the lottery.

She'd exclaimed, "That is so romantic!"

I frowned as she drew close. "Chris will be here any moment. You're not going to give him the Miss Eugeena talk?"

Mama grinned. "No! I just wanted to tell you to have fun tonight. Here, try this necklace on."

I recognized the gold heart necklace and teared up. "I can't wear that. Daddy gave that to you."

"Yes, your father gave this to me and now I'm passing it to you. He's not here, but I want you to remember he always wanted the best for you and for any man in your life to treat you right."

I took a deep breath. "Okay." I turned as Mama clasped the necklace around my neck.

"There you go. It's perfect."

I walked out into the hall to stand in front of the floor-length mirror. Mama was right. The heart sparkled against my skin, making my neck appear less naked.

My phone buzzed, and I slipped it out of my purse. A tiny panic seized my breath. I hoped it wasn't Chris calling to cancel. The crisis quickly evaporated when I read the text from Joss.

Get it, girl! Date #2! Thumbs up!

I sent her a smiling emoji.

Mama called out from the living room. "Looks like that's him turning into the driveway now. I will see you in the morning."

"Thanks, Mama. I appreciate you and Amos keeping the kids tonight." I closed the front door behind me as Chris's car pulled into the driveway. I walked toward the car so we weren't held up.

Even though our date had been a week ago, Chris had been by to see the kids, even picking them up earlier in the week when I had to work late. We were a co-parenting team. It had been hard all week to not gush about last week's dinner, which turned out to be a magical evening.

I only hoped date number two would go as well.

Chris climbed out of his car. Tonight, he dressed in a casual light blue button-down shirt and dark jeans. His smile was infectious, lighting up his face and making his eyes twinkle. "You look beautiful," he complimented as he opened the passenger door for me.

"Thank you," I replied. Heat rose to my cheeks as I climbed into the car. The scent of his cologne filled the air, comforting and familiar. "So, any hints about our destination?" I asked, hoping to pry some information from him.

"Nice try," Chris laughed, shaking his head. "You'll have to wait and see." He closed the passenger door.

As we drove through the city, I found myself lost in thought and nervous, again. Chris loved the older R&B music our parents listened to. That was something we both had in common, so I recognized the soothing voice of Luther Vandross.

“Leesa?” Chris’s concerned voice pulled me back to the present.

“Sorry,” I apologized, offering a small smile. “Were you saying something?”

“Just asking if Kisha did okay today. The other night she said a girl at camp was bothering her.”

I had noticed Kisha had been quiet earlier in the week. Her initial enthusiasm about attending camp seemed to go away. I figured she was just missing her grandmother. This was news to me.

“She told you that?”

Chris’s relationship with Kisha always amazed me. I wondered why she hadn’t mentioned it to me.

Chris continued. “Yeah, apparently this girl said some mean things to her when they were playing together. Kisha said she even pushed her.”

“Oh! Well, she knows to tell an adult. Did she tell anyone at the camp?”

“Let’s just keep an eye on it. I know about bullies. I dealt with a few in my time until I had my growth spurt.”

"I can imagine." Chris hadn't lost his football physique.

The sun dipped low in the sky, casting a golden glow on the nearly empty parking lot as Chris pulled up to a brick building. At first glance, it appeared to be a restaurant with double glass doors, but there were only three other cars.

"Okay, you've got me stumped," I admitted turning to Chris with a puzzled expression. "What's this place?"

"Ah, just wait and see," he answered. His eyes twinkled with mischief as he parked the car. He hopped out and quickly rounded the vehicle to open my door, holding out a hand to help me step out onto the pavement.

"Thank you," I said, taking his hand and feeling the familiar warmth of his touch. The gentle pressure of his fingers sent a shiver down my spine, reminding me of how much I missed this connection. We hadn't started the date yet, and already I wondered if we would share another kiss tonight.

I'd prayed this experiment would be successful because my flesh had been awakened like a sleeping giant.

After we entered through double glass doors, we stepped inside a modernly furnished lobby. A security guard sat behind a large counter. As we approached, the dark skinned man had a low cut silver afro and when he smiled, deep wrinkles creased around his eyes.

"Hey, Detective Black. Good to see you tonight."

"Good to see you as well, Henry. We'll head back."

Henry gave us a salute. "You both enjoy your evening."

Chris opened a door that led into a long hallway.

My curiosity piqued, I glanced over at Chris. "Are you going to tell me what we're doing here? How did you know the guard?"

"Patience, Leesa," he teased. "I promise you'll find out soon enough. And I met Henry a few weeks ago from a case."

After progressing a few more feet down the hall, we turned right. Then we walked through a set of double doors into a large, brightly lit room where three other couples sat classroom style. A familiar face stood behind a massive island with fresh ingredients. Recognition dawned on me as I realized it was a local chef I'd seen featured on the morning news.

Chef Dean Porter had a segment where he introduced meals that could be cooked in thirty minutes. I'd always wanted to try out his recipes but never had an opportunity. I'm sure I had quite a few written and bookmarked on my laptop.

A slim woman with huge glasses walked over to greet us with a clipboard in hand. I assumed she was an assistant. "Welcome, both of you," she said glancing down at her clipboard. "You are Chris Black?"

"Yes, and this is my lovely companion, Leesa Patterson."

Companion?

I tried hard not to raise my eyebrow. I wasn't sure how to absorb the label.

The assistant beamed. "It's an absolute pleasure to have both of you here tonight. Grab your table and put on your aprons."

Aprons?

Still not sure what was going on, I smiled. "I'm excited to be here."

I followed Chris to what was more like a small kitchen island than a table. Each couple sat on barstools at a similar setup.

I noticed the ingredients laid out, and that's when I realized.

We're cooking!

I looked over at Chris, who already had on his apron. Then I glanced down at my dress. *Man, did I overdress.*

Sensing my turmoil, Chris held out the apron. "Let's get this on you."

I slipped the apron over my head, glad that I'd pulled my hair back in the usual ponytail tonight. Chris quickly tied the apron in the back.

"Perfect," he murmured.

His breath on my neck had me feeling mushy again. I turned to focus on Chef Porter, giving Chris the side-eye with a grin.

This was definitely a different kind of date, but I applauded Chris for going all out with the effort.

"Tonight's class is all about creating chicken alfredo." Chef Porter's voice carried through the intimate cooking space. The walls were adorned with copper pots and pans hanging from rustic hooks, and the scent of garlic and onion filled the air. My stomach growled in anticipation. Chicken alfredo had always been a favorite dish of mine.

"Alright, let's get started," Chef Porter instructed. "One of you will slice the chicken, and the other can prep the pot for the sauce. Teamwork, ladies and gentlemen!"

Thanks to my mama, I had more experience in the kitchen than Chris, so it was an easy decision for him to slice the chicken. Chris's knife moved skillfully across the cutting board, his hands steady and confident. I couldn't help but sneak glances at him, admiring the way the muscles in his forearm flexed as he carefully sliced the chicken.

I stirred the butter and garlic in the pot. The rich aroma wafted up reminding me I hadn't eaten since lunch today.

"Alright, now that we've got our ingredients prepped, it's time to bring this dish together," Chef Porter interjected, guiding us through the next steps. As we cooked, the easy conversation continued, punctuated by laughter and gentle teasing.

"Almost there," Chris said as he stirred the alfredo sauce, a determined glint in his eyes. "Just a few more minutes, and we'll have a meal fit for a queen."

There was something profoundly intimate about creating a meal together, and I hoped this wouldn't be the last time we shared such a moment.

I was ravenous with hunger and all too happy when it was time to plate the chicken alfredo.

Chris twirled his fork inside the mound of pasta. "Let's see how we did."

I giggled, and then moaned as I tasted the velvety sauce coating the perfectly cooked pasta. The tender chicken melted in my mouth and I couldn't help but close my eyes and savor the moment. Then, I popped my eyes open, remembering we were out in public. To my delight, Chris had his eyes closed too.

"Mmmm, this is so good. We make a great team in the kitchen, don't you think?"

"Yeah, we do," I agreed before taking another bite.

We left the building walking hand in hand. This time it felt more natural than it did last week, as if we had always connected like this.

Before starting the car, Chris said softly. "Leesa, I'm determined to win you over." His eyes met mine with a vulnerability that made my heart ache. "I know I can't change the past, but I want to make up for it in any way I can."

"Chris, I…" My voice faltered as I struggled to find the words. His statement kind of floored me, reminding me he really was serious about making this work. There was a lot at stake for both of us.

My voice felt shaky as I blurted. "So far, so good. Two out of three isn't bad."

Chris chuckled. "Nice to know I'm scoring brownie points."

Despite my awkward response, I hoped Chris realized how much I wanted this to work out between us, too.

I clearly had fallen for him again.

Chapter 8

I twirled a strand of my curls absentmindedly around my finger, my mind burdened with worry. Three weeks had passed since our magical cooking class date, and once again, Chris's job as a detective took precedence. A series of shootings had claimed another young life, leaving a mother sonless. I'd been keeping up with the news and Chris's updates.

Chris rarely shared details with me, but this case had gotten under his skin. The mother's emotional pain had shaken him. He'd been so tired and discouraged lately. I prayed Chris and his partner would find the suspect responsible for the shooting. While I missed our time together, I knew what he needed more than anything was to be around the kids. They energized him.

"Leesa, are you okay?" my sister-in-law Carmen's face was etched with concern. She sat next to me on the couch, her eyes searching mine for answers. It was Saturday, and I knew how much my kids enjoyed Carmen and she them. So, I'd brought the kids over to visit. Carmen and my brother Cedric married a year ago but were still struggling to conceive.

I used to talk to Cedric, who I considered my favorite brother, about everything, especially after Dad died. My oldest brother, Junior, occasionally checked in with me. But he was so much older that he acted like more of a father figure than a brother. Since Cedric married, and I was close in age to his wife, I often sought her advice along with Joss's.

"I don't know, Carmen. I feel... discouraged. I understand Chris's job is important, but it's just so tough to keep getting my hopes up only for them to be shattered again. I mean, I guess this will be our lives if we were to get married."

Carmen gently responded. "Every relationship has its ups and downs, Leesa. Sometimes our choice of professions gets in the way. Your brother and I are doctors.

Some days we don't see each other. That's when we have to look at our schedules and make time for each other. You and Chris have something special. Let God work it out."

I forced a small smile. "You're right. I need to be more patient. It's just... hard, you know?"

"Of course it is." Carmen reached over to give me a hug. "But remember, you have people who love and support you no matter what. And if Chris is genuinely committed to making this work, he'll find a way."

Remembering our first two dates, the shared glances, whispered intentions and the way my hand felt in his, I said. "I believe he wants to make this work. I guess I just miss having the time together." I turned to Carmen. "I'm sorry. I'm over here whining about my love life. I know you and Cedric have been trying to have a baby for a while now. I know it's going to happen. Both of you are so good with kids, never mind that you deliver so many babies every year."

"I hope so. Having a little one will change our lives, but I'm looking forward to being a mom. Have you and Chris talked about the kids?"

"What do you mean?"

"Chris has always been there for them," Carmen continued. "Even when you weren't officially together. If you get hurt again, it might disrupt that balance for the children."

"I've thought about that too, Carmen," I confessed. "I just don't want to lose myself, you know?"

"Love is always a risk, Leesa. But you're strong, and I know both of you will make this work for you and your family."

My phone rang interrupting our conversation and offering a momentary relief from the heavy thoughts. I glanced at the screen. Butterflies fluttered in my stomach when I saw Chris's name.

"Hey, Leesa," Chris's voice came through, sounding tired but upbeat. "We cracked the case. Suspect is in custody."

My heart leaped in my chest. "That's wonderful news!"

Chris cleared his throat. "Yeah, I was wondering if you'd like to join me for a party tonight? I could use the break."

"Is this our third date, finally?" I joked, trying to keep my tone light even as my mind raced.

"Ha, no, not exactly," Chris replied with a chuckle. "It's just a casual gathering with family. I thought it might be nice to spend some time together and hang out with some other people."

"Alright," I agreed hesitantly, looking at Carmen, who offered an encouraging nod. "I'll see you in a couple hours, then."

"Great. Hey, dress comfortable," Chris said before hanging up.

I put down my phone and a mixture of excitement and anxiety coursed through me. Tonight would be another opportunity to reconnect with Chris. But a nagging doubt crept in, threatening to overshadow the sweet memories of our first two dates.

I smoothed the fabric of my dark denim skirt, which I had paired with a white top. I knew I was probably taking a chance wearing white, but at least I wasn't as dressy as I was for the cooking class. I also wore the necklace Mama gave me. I tried to give it back to her, but she was serious about me keeping it. I pulled the heart locket down so it laid in the center right above the v-shape of the shirt.

I applied a touch of lip gloss, and then slipped into my brown open-toe sandals. I got a pedicure after work yesterday so I was sporting pale pink shimmering toe polish. Not too bad, even though this was not the infamous third date. But I was Chris's plus one to this party, which had me concerned.

Wear something comfortable were his instructions earlier on the phone. The only other detail he added was it was a family event. Though it was nice to be introduced to his family as a couple again, I really wanted the extra time together.

Alone.

Cedric and Carmen kept the kids for a sleepover tonight. I was lucky to have family and friends who were there for me. Despite my breaking things off with Chris a few years back and moving back to Charleston, the support system alone did wonders for my mental health.

The sound of a car horn outside signaled Chris's arrival, and I took one last deep breath. When I opened the door, Chris waited outside the door dressed even more casually in a polo shirt and jeans.

"You ready?"

"Sure." I reached for the front door to close and lock it. "So, what is this family event about?"

"My cousin Jamal's birthday party," Chris explained as he opened the car door for me. "I thought it would be fun."

"Oh," I almost paused before climbing into the car. "Well, there will be cake and good food." I smiled, but those lingering doubts from earlier wrapped around my throat.

I would rather spend time with Chris's mom than attend Jamal's party. Belinda Black was at least polite in her own way. Jamal was rough around the edges, like really rough. I often wondered how Chris, being in law enforcement, kept his relationship with his cousin, who definitely had seen a jail cell a few times.

Chris started the engine. "But don't worry, I promise this isn't our official third date. We used to hang out at parties back in the day."

"Yeah. But just remember parties are not my thing. I've just never been good at that mingling thing."

Chris touched my knee. "It will be fine, I promise. I won't leave your side."

His warm hand on my bare knee warmed me, but it didn't quiet my nerves. I knew what to expect. I hadn't drunk alcohol since high school and sometimes it made me uncomfortable, bringing back bad memories. I had my moments as a teen hanging with a bad crowd, which included Kisha's dad. But as soon as I delivered Kisha, I changed my ways, realizing I had just been acting out of grief and rebellion from losing my best friend.

As the car pulled away, I forced myself to focus on the positive. Tonight was an opportunity for Chris and me to show each other — and the world — that we were a couple again.

"That's a pretty necklace. You wore it the last time we were out." Chris commented.

I touched it. "It's my mom's. My dad gave it to her not too long before he died."

"Wow! That's pretty special."

"Yeah, I was surprised when she gave it to me."

"I miss my dad every day. He would have loved to be here tonight. My dad loved to be on the grill. I wished I had time to get some of his skills before he passed."

I thought about my dad as I fiddled with the heart necklace. My mood had dipped considerably more by the time Chris pulled up to a house that looked more like a parking lot in the front. Once I stepped out of the car, the lively sounds of laughter and hip-hop music spilled out onto the street.

I took a deep breath, trying to calm my racing heart.

"Hey, don't worry," Chris grabbed my hand. "We'll stick together, okay? And if it gets too overwhelming, we can always step outside for some fresh air."

"Thanks," I said, feeling reassured by the grip of his hand. Together, we moved through the crowded living room where Chris stopped to introduce me to various relatives. I'd met some of them over the years. Each warm embrace and sincere smile from his loved ones made me feel more at ease.

"See?" Chris murmured into my ear as we shared a quiet moment in a corner of the room. "I told you it wouldn't be so bad."

"No, not bad. Is your mom here?"

Chris shook his head. "No, she never comes to parties, especially since Dad died. My aunts are always asking about her, though. We should head out back and grab some food."

After eating a burger and slaw, my full belly helped me settle into the party. I didn't even mind chatting with Jamal for a while. It was his birthday and despite my feelings about him, I knew Chris looked up to him like a big brother. The music had been blasting since we arrived, but a few couples made a makeshift dance floor in the middle of the living room. People moved out of the way to watch the dancers.

Next thing I knew, Chris pulled me forward, and our bodies swayed gently to the slow rhythm of a classic by Goapele, "Closer." I allowed myself to melt into his embrace, feeling the warmth of his body against mine was a familiar comfort I hadn't realized how much I had missed. Chris pulled me closer as we continued to sway to the music. For those few fleeting moments, everything felt perfect - just Chris and me.

The song ended and a more upbeat tune played, drawing more people onto the dance floor. I giggled because I knew we'd finally reached a limit. Chris conceded. "I can't compete with your killer dance moves."

"You never could," I teased. I hadn't danced in a long time, but I could move when the music hit me.

"Guilty as charged," he responded, raising his hands in surrender. So far, my doubts had been unfounded. Despite this not being the third date, it had been a lot of fun.

But as quickly as the thought formed, it dissipated when a familiar figure entered the room.

Isis Malone.

Chris's ex-girlfriend.

What was she doing here?

I watched as Isis went over to Jamal, giving him a hug. Jamal whispered something in her ear, and then she turned. Her dark curls framed her face as she scanned the crowd. I knew the second she locked eyes with Chris. I felt his body stiffen next to me. Without hesitation, she made her way toward him, her stride confident and purposeful.

"Chris," she called, her voice tinged with a sense of urgency. "I'm so glad you're here. I need to talk to you."

It was like she didn't even see me standing next to him. An icy sensation crept down my spine as a knot of unease formed in the pit of my stomach. When I glanced at Chris, my body grew warm. He seemed equally taken aback by Isis's sudden appearance.

His eyes met mine for a moment, and I saw his confusion. But I wanted him to reject her. She couldn't just barge in and demand his time.

"Uh, sure," he responded hesitantly, his brow furrowing in concern. He turned to me, his face oddly blank. "Give me a minute, okay?"

Stunned, I heard myself murmur, "Take your time." I swallowed the lump in my throat as I watched Chris and Isis retreat out of the living room. I didn't know this house, so I had no idea where they went. I couldn't help but wonder what this unexpected encounter would mean for our fragile reunion.

I tried not to seem impatient for Chris and Isis to return, but I couldn't ignore the growing sense of unease that gnawed at me ever since Chris asked me to come to this party out of the blue. I looked around and noticed Jamal staring at me.

Was that a smirk on his face?

"Hey," a soft voice broke through my racing thoughts, and I looked up to see Chris returning to my side. His expression was guarded. "I'm really sorry about that, Leesa. I wasn't expecting her to be here."

Noticing that people were watching us, I forced a tight smile on my face. "What did she want?"

Chris hesitated for a moment, his gaze flickering across the crowd. "It's... complicated."

"Complicated?" I echoed. My pulse quickened as the knot in my stomach tightened. "How so?"

"I'd rather not talk about it here," he said evasively, his hand brushing against mine to offer comfort. "Can we discuss it on the way home?"

"Fine," I agreed, though my unease remained.

A deafening silence filled the car on the ride back, the tension between us palpable. I had so many questions that burned inside me.

Why was Isis here? Did he really not know she was in Charleston?

I felt Chris' eyes on me as if he was waiting for me to lash out. It's what I did years ago, I screamed and cried from his betrayal. But we weren't in a moving car either.

So, it wasn't until Chris parked in the driveway that I finally found the courage to speak. "Chris, I don't think we should continue this relationship."

"Wait, what?" he stammered, his eyes widening in shock as he turned to face me. "Leesa, give me a chance to explain. I just need to process first."

"Process what? Your ex showed up tonight. The one you spent years with ... the one that was in our way before. Why is she even in Charleston?"

I held up my hand.

I didn't want to know.

"Tonight, seeing Isis again made me realize something," I confessed with my hands fumbling for the door handle. "I don't think you're over her, Chris. She asked to speak to you and you were standing right next to me. And you just went off to talk to her. How do you think that made me feel?"

"Leesa, I'm sorry ..." he pleaded. His voice was raw with emotion as he reached for my hand. "Isis means nothing to me anymore. It's you I want to be with."

But I shook my head, tears pricking the corners of my eyes. "I can't take that chance, Chris. My heart couldn't handle it and neither could our kids if we end up falling apart again."

"Leesa, I promise—" he began, but I cut him off.

"Goodbye, Chris," I murmured before stepping out of the car into the humid night air. I didn't look back as I made my way up the steps, my heart heavy with the weight of my decision.

Chris didn't even try to follow me. He just started the car and screeched out of the driveway.

Inside, I leaned against the door, sliding down onto the cold floor as tears finally spilled over, and silent sobs shook my body. Despite the pain, I knew it was for the best. We were doing fine as we were. But the ache in my chest told me Chris and I couldn't go back. So I sat on the floor mourning the loss of what might have been.

Chapter 9

My brother dropped the kids off after church. Cedric joked. "You must have had a good time last night. You missed church, which you know you will hear about from Mama."

I sighed. "I know. Tell Carmen thank you again for keeping the kids."

Cedric crossed his arms. "Sure. Everything okay with you and Chris?"

In his stance, Cedric looked every bit like my dad. He was the spitting image of Ralph Patterson, Sr. I knew my brother meant well, and there was a time I would have spilled to him about some guy doing me wrong, but somehow I felt not mentioning last night was a better idea.

"All good!" I quickly asked the Lord for forgiveness.

Missed church and now lying. Great start to the week, Leesa.

After I shooed Cedric out of the house, my phone buzzed. My heart jolted. Chris had left a message, but I hadn't bothered to listen to the voicemail. I didn't want to hear his voice.

Thankfully, it was a text from Joss.

Joss: Hey, Leesa, you doing okay? I'm here for you, girl.

I smiled faintly, grateful for her unwavering support. I needed to vent to someone about the party. So after I picked myself up off the floor last night, I'd called Joss. Sometimes you needed someone else to tell you if you were doing the right thing or not.

My fingers glided over the phone as I typed.

Leesa: Thanks, Joss. Just trying to figure things out.

Joss: I know. But don't you want to know what they talked about?

My fingers hovered over my phone, uncertainty clouding my thoughts. Did I really want to hear the details of Chris's conversation with Isis? I convinced myself last night it was better not to know. But now curiosity gnawed at my insides, refusing to be ignored.

Leesa: Maybe.

I typed slowly, knowing Joss was probably annoyed at seeing the ellipses on her end as I tried to form a response. I had grown pretty annoyed with myself.

Leesa: I just don't know if I can handle it right now.

Joss: Take your time, but don't let that woman steal Chris from you again.

If I wasn't hurting so, I would laugh. Joss had a way of being abrupt, which I appreciated about her.

Leesa: Thanks, Joss.

I could hear Kisha fussing at Tyric about something and knew I needed to go check on them. As I made my way to their bedrooms, I thought about how Chris would swoop in and make things better when the kids were at each other. Kids just listened to a man differently compared to their mother sometimes.

In the last few weeks, Chris appeared more like the man I'd fallen in love with all those years ago, not just a loving father, but a caring partner. But now the shadow of Isis loomed large, threatening to shatter the fragile romance we'd been trying to rebuild in the last month. In my heart, I knew I needed to confront this head-on, get to the truth of why she was even in Charleston.

But fear held me back.

Tuesday after work, I busied myself with tidying up when Chris called to say he would arrive in twenty minutes. It had been three days since the party. Despite my anger about him talking to Isis, my heart raced with anticipation knowing that Chris was coming by to see the kids. I knew I probably could have eased the tension that had grown between us by hearing him out, but I didn't want to hear about Isis.

No amount of curiosity would allow me to break my stubbornness about the matter.

"Mommy, when will Daddy be here?" Kisha asked. Her little eyes filled with excitement. Chris didn't come by on Sunday like he normally would have, and Mondays were usually busy for him.

"Any minute now, sweetie," I replied, forcing a smile. Chris seemed okay with Kisha calling him daddy even though he wasn't her biological father. I told him she could just call him Chris, but he said that wouldn't be right. Truly, he'd been the only father figure Kisha had known.

When the doorbell rang, Kisha raced toward the door with Tyric right on her heels. I peeked at the app on my phone to make sure it was Chris at the door, and then promptly snuck off toward the bedroom. I knew hiding was childish, but I didn't want to interfere with Chris's time with the kids, so I listened from behind my door.

"Hey, munchkins!" Chris's voice boomed as he entered. His infectious laughter filled the room. The children's giggles sounded bittersweet in my ears, I wanted to be in the mix too.

"Where's your mama?"

"Umm, she's...busy," Kisha said hesitantly.

I cringed, feeling bad about having my eight-year-old telling tales about her mama. I knew she could sense something was wrong, but I told her what to say if Chris asked for me.

"Alright," I heard Chris reply, a hint of disappointment in his voice. "Let's go outside and play."

He knew I was purposely avoiding him. It was my way of handling my emotions when I really wanted to fly off the handle at him. I didn't want the kids to see me that upset.

After I heard them outside in the backyard, I tiptoed to my bedroom window to peek through the curtains. I took a step back from the curtain when I saw Chris look toward the window.

Please don't come in here to talk to me.

I strained my neck to observe him hesitate for a moment as if debating whether to come looking for me. But then, he turned his attention to the kids, tossing a ball into the air for them to catch.

I sighed and moved away from the window. I knew Chris wanted to talk about what happened between him and Isis. I couldn't get past him leaving me standing there alone while he went to talk to *her*. It was beyond humiliating.

I sat on my bed and drummed my fingers in a steady rhythm on the cool wooden surface of my nightstand. My heart pounded in sync with each tap, echoing another thought that had been tormenting me.

Was I just being jealous?

A nagging voice in my head whispered that I was indeed experiencing the green eyed monster and had overreacted as a result.

I needed to get it together.

We couldn't keep going on like this.

Wednesday lived up to its name, hump day. My tasks were pretty monotonous, which allowed my mind to wander. A few years ago when I started seeing a therapist, she mentioned my tendency to run and hide when things got tough. When I didn't want to deal with an issue, I tried hard to bury my head in the sand. Guilt and shame would sit right beside me, like two old toxic friends, keeping me chained in place.

I was glad Mama didn't call me about missing church on Sunday. I would have been compelled to tell her what happened. Somewhere in that conversation, she would have asked me what happened to my faith and had I been praying.

I had been praying ... for a long time.

I wanted a full family which included a husband, too. Someone I could wake up beside and be there all the time to help with the kids. Like that cooking class, I wanted to have moments in the kitchen with Chris cooking beside me. I didn't want the kids over with me and then over at his place.

In some ways, I felt like I'd been given a test and failed. That same insecure woman who broke up with Chris years ago hadn't changed at all. I did what I did the last time. I didn't think of myself as a woman fighting for her man. If he wanted her, he could have her–that had been my decision. But this time, things were different. The stakes were higher, and I couldn't let Isis swoop in and snatch away the life I'd worked so hard to build with Chris and our children.

I took a breath and moved my chair back from my desk. The torrent of thoughts had me more emotional than I needed to be at work. I leaned over to grab my bag from my desk drawer, seeing that it would be lunch time soon. I frowned as I noticed my phone seemed to be receiving a call. I kept my phone on silent while at work. Most people in my life never called me during work hours. Even Mama just sent a text if she needed to send me a message.

The caller ID displayed Kisha's camp, and my heart skipped a beat. I swiped to answer, my voice shaking slightly. "Hello?"

My fingers clenched around the phone, every breath hitched in my chest as I listened to the nurse's voice on the other end. "Thank goodness. Ms. Patterson, we've been trying to reach you. This is the nurse from Camp Willow. We had to take Kisha to the emergency room. She fell and hurt her arm."

"Is she alright?" I asked, my voice wavering with concern.

"Her arm may be broken, but we won't know for sure until the doctor examines her," the nurse replied, her tone professional yet gentle. "She's in good hands, Ms. Patterson. The hospital is only a few miles away from our camp."

After obtaining the name of the hospital, I managed to say thank you. My heart was pounding in my chest. Mind wracked with fear, I ended the call and rushed down the hallway to my boss's office. My thoughts were a whirlwind as I struggled to focus on how Kisha could get hurt. I trusted the camp to take care of my child.

"Mr. Thompson, I'm so sorry, but I have an emergency," I blurted out as I entered his office. "My daughter's in the hospital. I need to go."

"Go, Leesa. Family comes first. Keep me updated."

"Thank you," I murmured.

I raced to my car, the world around me a blur. As I sped through the streets, my thoughts turned to Kisha, my quiet, little helper. She often appeared older than her age. The nurse assured me she was fine. But Kisha had never been in the hospital before, so I knew my firstborn must be scared.

My body trembled as the entrance doors to the emergency room slid open. The overhead lighting cast a harsh glow on the linoleum floor, making everything feel surreal and disjointed. I approached the nurses' station, barely able to keep my tongue from tying over my words. "My daughter, Kisha Patterson, was injured at camp. They brought her here."

"Yes, can you show me your ID?"

I fumbled in my purse, pulling my ID and insurance card from the wallet. Finally, the nurse took me back. When she pulled the curtains back, Kisha's sweet voice greeted me. "Mama!"

Relief washed over me in waves as I saw her sitting on a hospital bed. Her left arm was wrapped in a makeshift sling and an ice pack was pressed against her elbow. Tears welled up in my eyes, but I blinked them back not wanting Kisha to see how scared I was.

"Munchkin," I whispered, rushing over and pulling her into a gentle hug. "Are you okay?" I asked examining her arm.

"Leesa." Chris's warm voice broke through the haze of emotion. So focused on seeing Kisha, I hadn't even noticed Chris. He sat near Kisha's bed, concern etched into the lines of his face. "The camp kept trying to contact you. They got me instead and I got here as soon as I could. The nurse said it might be a fracture, but they're taking her for x-rays soon."

"Thank you, Chris," I murmured. My gratefulness for his support overrode any of my previous feelings. They didn't even matter.

"Mama, Daddy made me laugh when I was crying," Kisha piped up, her small face bright.

"Did he now?" I glanced at Chris, my heart swelling with love for this man who had always been there for our children, no matter what. He shrugged modestly.

"Yup! Mama, why did the cookie go to the doctor?" Kisha giggled, the sound like music to my ears.

I grinned, thinking I had heard this one before. "Why did the cookie go?"

Kisha giggled so hard she could barely say the punch line. "Because he was feeling crummy." Suddenly tired, Kisha said softly, "Mama?"

"Yes, baby." I rubbed her knee.

"I feel crummy too."

"I know. You keep being a big girl. You will feel better soon."

Kisha looked over at Chris, and then back at me.

That's when I realized how awkward it must have seemed to Kisha that I would hide from Chris when he came over.

Considering today's events, I felt pretty silly. The tension between Chris and me seemed to dissipate, replaced by a united front for Kisha.

I took a deep breath and let my eyes linger on Chris for a moment, silently promising him I wouldn't give up on us so easily this time. He returned my gaze, reminding me he loved my daughter, his son and he loved me, too.

Chapter 10

The next day, after getting the truth from Kisha, we found out she hadn't just fallen. She had been pushed. Her arm wasn't broken, but fractured. A united force, Chris and I berated both the camp counselor and the parents of the girl who pushed Kisha. There were no complaints from Kisha when we pulled her out of the camp. I believe she preferred spending the rest of her summer with Grandma Eugeena and Grandpa Amos anyway.

While things had settled down on the home front, there were still some things to settle between me and Chris. I finally opened my mind to his conversation with Isis. We needed to move past it, or at least I did.

Chris brought dinner from the Chicken Shack, which included wings for us and chicken nuggets for the kids. Together, we'd settled them both in the bed after baths.

I joined Chris in the living room where he sat on the couch. Feeling awkward I stood a few feet away. I knew I needed to start the long overdue conversation. "Thanks for going to the hospital to be with Kisha. I had my phone on silent, but it's not usually in my bag either. I'm thankful we had you down as an emergency contact too."

He looked at me warily. "Of course."

I sucked in a breath. "I'm sorry for overreacting on Saturday night."

Chris patted the cushion beside him, beckoning me to come sit on the couch with him. I shuffled over and sat on the edge of the seat.

"I need to apologize to you."

My back stiffened. "Why?"

"Isis had been trying to reach out to me for a few days, but I ignored her calls and messages. I didn't expect her to show up here in Charleston."

I could feel the tension rise in my body, but I pressed further. "So, what did she want to talk to you about?"

"I learned too late that Isis likes to use people."

My eyes widened in shock. "What do you mean?"

Chris rubbed his hand across his low cut hair and sighed. "It turns out that Isis's brother got into some trouble with the law and she thought I could help him out. She caught me off guard because I know her brother. He has always been a decent guy. Jamal was the one who gave her the idea. I don't know what he thought he was doing by having her show up at his birthday party."

I felt my stomach sicken as the implications slowly sank in. "I guess Jamal doesn't like me either. He certainly looked at me like he knew it would hurt me."

Chris shook his head. "I'm sorry, Leesa. You know my mom warned me about certain folks on my dad's side of the family. There's a reason she doesn't hang out with them. I should have known something was up the way Jamal hounded me to come. In all honesty, he didn't know we were back together, but it still wasn't right for him to invite Isis, either. Everything happened so fast, and I know I reacted wrong. I just wanted to get rid of her. I promise, my feelings are for you only."

"I'm sorry for reacting the way I did. I thought I'd moved past all that."

Chris reached out for my hand. "I put you in a bad situation, especially when I know you don't like parties. And Isis showing up wasn't cool. I probably would have reacted the same way."

I squeezed his hand, feeling a wave of relief wash over me. "It's in the past now. So, what happened with Isis's brother?"

Chris let out a bitter laugh. "Turns out he was guilty after all. I wouldn't have been able to help him even if I wanted to."

I shook my head, feeling a mix of frustration and sadness. "What a mess."

Chris nodded in agreement. "Yeah. But we can move on and focus on building our own future together."

I laughed. "So, there really is a third date?"

"Absolutely. This time, I want you to decide what you want to do. I realize I've sprung a lot of surprises on you."

I put my hand on my chest. "I get to decide what we do."

Chris gave me a sly smile. "I'm at your mercy. Oh, by the way, you dropped this in the car, and I wanted to hand it to you personally."

I frowned as Chris pulled something out of his shirt pocket.

And then gasped when I realized it was the heart necklace. "Oh, my goodness, Chris. Mama gave that to me and I hadn't realized I lost it."

"Not lost, just misplaced. Let me put it back on you."

My heart beat a mile a minute. In all my turmoil over the Isis situation, I'd not paid attention to something so small and precious. As Chris fastened the necklace on me, tears sprang to my eyes. I'd almost lost this precious gift from my dad.

Chris turned me around and cupped my chin. Then he wiped the tears that escaped down my face. "Hey, we're okay. And maybe this is a way of your dad looking down on you."

Not able to speak, I nodded.

Chris embraced me and I clung to him, not wanting to let go.

I thanked my Father God and my daddy, who I knew watched over me from heaven.

I was still a daddy's girl!

I thought about what I wanted to do for our third date. Even though Chris and I were both native Charlestonians, I decided we needed to really experience our hometown. There were awesome experiences right under our noses.

So, approximately a month after our first date, butterflies danced in my stomach as I waited for Chris. Even though Mama and Amos had the kids all day, she volunteered to keep them overnight. I wore the necklace from Daddy. This time I paired it with a flowy white dress with pink flowers that stopped just above my knees.

Chris arrived right on time. When I opened the door, he greeted me with a wide smile. Dressed in light gray slacks and a white button-down shirt, he looked dapper as always.

"You look gorgeous. Oh, and these are for you."

I hadn't noticed that he had his hands behind his back. He pulled out a bouquet of daffodils.

"Oh, my favorites, Chris! How sweet! Let me put these in water." The butterflies in my stomach swarmed as the fragrance of the flowers tantalized my nose. It was a sweet nervousness.

Tonight would be perfect.

I could feel it in my spirit.

As normal, we chatted about our day on the ride over. Unlike the other two times, I knew where we were going. I'd mentioned my idea to Chris last night, and he was all in. It occurred to me the other night that we'd not experienced all the fine dining Charleston offered.

Chris found a parking space, and then grabbed my hand as we walked toward the building. The temperatures were still warm, but there was a slight breeze coming from the ocean as we approached.

As we stepped onto the rooftop restaurant, my breath hitched in my throat. The sun had already started its descent on the horizon. The sky was a beautiful mix of reds and oranges.

Chris squeezed my hand and chuckled. "You did good. Nice view!"

After we were seated at a table, I marveled over this different view of the Charleston harbor, grateful for my hometown.

The food was amazing. I almost didn't want the night to end.

Apparently, Chris didn't either because we didn't head back to the car like I expected.

His eyes twinkled. "Sorry, I couldn't resist another surprise."

I opened my mouth to protest, but shut it quickly when I saw where we were heading.

"Really! A horse-drawn carriage ride." All the years I lived here, I'd seen tourists and even wedding parties riding in these carriages, but never thought about riding in one myself. I felt like a princess being escorted by her Prince Charming.

We cuddled next to each other on the seat and watched as the horses trotted down cobblestone streets in front of us with their manes blowing in the wind. The beauty of Charleston surrounded us on all sides as the night grew darker and stars filled the sky above us like twinkling diamonds.

"Leesa," Chris spoke my name softly in my ear. "I have something for you."

That's when I saw a small box in his hands. My heart skipped a beat as I realized what was happening.

He opened the box and revealed a beautiful sparkling diamond ring. "Leesa, will you marry me?"

Tears of joy sprung to my eyes. "Yes."

Chris slid the ring on my finger. Then he leaned down and kissed me gently on the lips. I kissed him back, feeling a flood of emotions and gratefulness that we'd finally reached this point in our journey.

Trust in the Lord, He will grant the desires of your heart.

Author's Note

During the pandemic, book clubs invited me virtually to meet for discussions about *Deep Fried Trouble*, the first book in the Eugeena Patterson Mysteries. It soon became apparent to me that many readers were concerned about the relationship between Leesa Patterson and Chris Black. I started writing *Deep Fried Trouble* in 2008, but didn't publish it until 2013. So focused on developing the main character, I hadn't realized I'd painted a picture of Chris Black that would leave an imprint on the minds of readers.

Chris appeared rough and menacing, when in fact he was still trying to figure out who he was, just like his girlfriend Leesa Patterson. In their early twenties, both had suffered similar losses of their father and experienced relationships that left them tainted. After having their son, Leesa struggled not only with postpartum depression, but with grief and her own insecurities.

With every book in the Eugeena Patterson Mysteries, I always feel compelled to bring back recurring characters, specifically Eugeena's children and their significant others. It's the moments when Eugeena is around her family where I feel like I'm able to fully develop her character outside the mystery. The Eugeena Patterson Family Shorts have been a way to introduce these family dynamics.

I'm so delighted that you read *Falling For You Again.* I promise that you will see more of Leesa and Chris in the Eugeena Patterson Mysteries. I already have a book in the works where Eugeena and Leesa join forces to solve a crime together.

Lookout, Chris and Amos!

In the meantime, on the next few pages, you can read more about that long-awaited honeymoon trip that Eugeena and Amos had returned from earlier in this story. Grab your copy of ***A Spicy Predicament***.

A Spicy Predicament

Eugeena Patterson Mysteries, Book 6

Eugeena Patterson-Jones and her husband, Amos Jones, finally head out for their long-awaited honeymoon in Music City. As part of a surprise, Eugeena is treated to a concert starring one of her favorite singers. Cinnamon Waters, also a childhood friend, invites Eugeena and Amos backstage. Behind the glitz and music, tension brews and Eugeena will find out someone wants to harm Cinnamon.

When one mishap after the other keeps happening, the couple's romantic getaway takes a backseat to trying to save her friend's life.

Chapter 1

I think I've swayed my hips more in my old age than when I was younger.

Eugeena, you still got it, girl!

The man in front of me wasn't moving too bad either. Amos Jones had his two step game going strong like a man twenty years younger. Even with the lights shimmering off his bald head, I could picture how good looking he'd been back in the day. He was still handsome in my book. Aged like fine wine!

We had finally embarked on the honeymoon we should have taken over a year ago. Why so long? Well, certain events delayed our breakaway from our daily life. And there were the unexpected mysteries that I'd been determined to solve. But a sistah had grown tired of coming across people who committed unspeakable acts of evil, like murder. I'd experienced many melancholy days and a few nightmares that stole my sleep at night.

The amateur sleuth hobby had not been how I planned to spend my retirement years.

Tonight, the blues permeated the air, but I was quite giddy. An incredible feat, seeing as I was 550 miles away from my beloved home. I had spent all my life in Charleston, South Carolina, where I was born and raised. The most visited city in South Carolina, I'd seen people from all over the world in my hometown, but I'd not traveled much outside the palmetto state. I loved my Sugar Creek neighborhood where I'd spent more than half my life raising kids, being married to my first husband and in the past few years meeting my new hubby.

Amos proposed driving up to Music City, but I didn't see myself sitting in the car for eight hours. We were way too old for that. Conquering my trepidation for flying, we made it to Nashville, Tennessee, yesterday afternoon. I hated I missed church, but Amos caught a good deal on our flight out of the Charleston International Airport.

Today, after a morning of sightseeing, and an afternoon nap, we were now, to Amos's amusement, hanging out in what I called a juke joint. The Blue Note

Lounge, in fact, was very sophisticated with its textured walls, cushy seats, and mahogany tables. It was certainly no hole in the wall, not that I knew much about those kind of places.

The Blue Note's walls were lined with portraits of musicians, both famous and local. Although it was called the Blue Note, tonight we'd heard everything from Motown classics to jazz. While the lounge band wrapped up a lively number of songs, Amos held his hand on the small of my back, guiding us back to our table. I wasn't sure how we were lucky enough to be seated near the stage. In the corner to our right was an old jukebox. In between the band sets, someone would push buttons keeping the atmosphere festive.

Now that we were seated, I had a chance to see the beautiful singer dressed in a dazzling red dress. She'd delighted the crowd and was ending her set with "What a Difference A Day Makes," which I recognized as one of my mama's favorite songs. Mama loved Dinah Washington. One of the few things I remembered about her.

Our server swung by. Her big smile lit up a round face. She wore her hair in box braids that were swept up on top of her head.

"Y'all want your drinks refilled?"

While others were drinking spirits, I wasn't trying to be too adventurous. Besides, I wasn't an alcohol drinker, the taste never appealed to me. The Blue Note Lounge served food, and I had a tall, sweet tea with a basket of some of the best chicken fingers I'd had. Just enough spice to ignite my senses, but not too much to leave me up with heartburn later. The server poured more tea for me and brought Amos another craft beer.

"Ladies and gentlemen, can I have your attention?" I peered toward the stage. A young man had walked out on the stage, his white smile dazzling in the spotlight. I'd noticed the standard dress at the Blue Note Lounge seemed to be a black shirt, black jeans, and cowboy boots. There was an older announcer who introduced singing acts throughout the evening, but something about the younger announcer felt familiar to me.

He continued. "The person you've been waiting to see is ready to hit the stage. She's a favorite here at the

Blue Note." Then he pointed to the crowd. "Are you ready?"

I bellowed out "Yeah," like the others around me. I'd been looking forward to this ever since Amos showed me the two tickets he purchased. After so many years, I would finally get to see a childhood friend.

Cinnamon Waters.

Cinnamon stepped onto the stage as the crowd roared with excitement. Cinnamon and I were the same age, but she seemed much younger than me, defying her sixty-three years. Her elegant afro puff was pinned back with a large red bow. She wore a short, sparkly dress that hugged her curves in all the right places. How was she able to keep that figure? I sure would like to know. She smiled and waved at the audience.

"How y'all doing out there?" As her name implied, Cinnamon's voice was sweet with a touch of spice. "So good to have you here. I have a few of my favorites I'd like to share. How does that sound?"

The audience responded in one accord.

The guitar player started a few chords followed by the rest of the band. As Cinnamon sang, her voice was just as I remembered when we were girls in the choir. Now it was more powerful, more soulful, and full of emotion. As she sang, Cinnamon moved with the rhythm of the music, slowly swaying her shoulders and throwing her head back. Cinnamon's sultry voice mesmerized people from all ages and races.

By Cinnamon's second set, the crowd seemed to have grown around us. I hadn't paid attention to all the tables filling in. I assumed it was a pretty good crowd for a Monday evening.

I felt so proud of my friend. This woman was one of my closest friends at one time. Back then, she was shy and timid. But there was no sign of that young girl tonight.

Cinnamon asked, "Can you bring up the house lights? I want to see who's with us tonight." The overhead lights slowly flickered on across the lounge. She walked to the edge of the stage and patted her glistening face with a handkerchief. "Ah, yes, you all look beautiful."

Cinnamon placed her hand over her eyes to shade them as she scanned the room. To my surprise, our eyes met.

She pointed at me. “I see a special friend is here tonight.”

I grinned and waved.

She sauntered over to the stage nearest to our table. “It’s so good to have you here, Eugeena. This next song is for you, my dear friend.”

I grabbed Amos’s hand, tears filling my eyes. I whispered, “How did she know I was here?”

Amos winked like he had a secret.

To my surprise, Cinnamon sang “Amazing Grace,” her voice washing over me like warm water. As she sang, I closed my eyes, envisioning sweet memories from our childhood. This was a song Cinnamon’s late mother used to sing. After she finished the song, she blew me a kiss. The crowd cheered and clapped, and I blew her a kiss back.

Cinnamon disappeared behind the curtains. The young man who had announced her showed up at our table. “Eugeena Patterson.”

"Yes."

"Ms. Waters wanted me to give you a backstage tour."

"What?" I looked over at Amos. "Did you know about this?"

Amos grinned. "I've been busy over the past few weeks. You were worried about what I was doing. Told you I was making plans."

My hubby may have outdone himself. In all honesty, I was grateful to see Cinnamon onstage, but she was a world traveler, and it'd been some years since we last saw each other. In fact, the last time I saw her was six years ago at my late husband Ralph Patterson's funeral.

We rose from the table and followed the young man. I couldn't help but be nosy. Something about the young man seemed familiar. "Are you related to Cinnamon?"

He turned and smiled. "She's my grandma."

I sucked in a breath as another memory hit me. "I knew it. You remind me of her younger brother."

The man nodded. "Uncle Charlie. Yeah, I get that a lot. Too bad I never got to meet him."

"Yes, it's a shame. He was quite the musician."

"I heard. I play the piano like he did. Do a little singing too."

"Runs in the family." As we entered the backstage, my thoughts went to Charlie Waters. He was my earliest crush. All the hours we spent playing out in the country, you get to know people, and there was no one as funny and rambunctious as Charlie. Charlie unfortunately passed many years ago before we all graduated from high school. "What's your name, son?"

"Jared."

"That's a nice name. You say you are a singer, too?"

Jared smiled. "I used to sing, but I mainly help manage my grandma's gigs."

Used to sing. He's so young.

"That's beautiful that you're helping out your grandma."

Going back behind the stage was a whole new experience for me. It was a tight squeeze. And a lot of people were standing around. I recognized some members of Cinnamon's band and her two backup singers. As we passed by, I noticed one of the backup singers and one of the band members, the guitar player, I think, were not too happy about something.

Could've been my suspicious nature, but the woman appeared scared and moved her hands around erratically. I caught the man grabbing her arms as if to steady her. I didn't have time to see anymore before Jared stopped in front of a door labeled "Dressing Room."

Jared knocked on the door, and then frowned. His hand stilled on the doorknob.

I listened closely. Someone was in there with Cinnamon.

The deepness of the voice indicated it was probably a man.

Their voices were raised, and though I couldn't tell what they were saying, it sounded like a full on argument to me.

I glanced at Jared and noticed his smile had disappeared. Deep lines marred the young man's forehead and his body seemed to grow stiff as a board.

An odd familiar feeling crept up my spine. Over the past few years, I'd developed a sense when something bad was going to happen. Amos told me it came from my witnessing how people treat other people during their darkest moments.

As the voices grew louder, I quickly prayed for peace and that I was wrong about a storm approaching.

Click here to read more or go to https://books2read.com/aspicypredicament

About the Author

Tyora Moody is the author of **Soul-Searching Mysteries,** which includes **cozy mystery, women sleuth mystery, and mystery romance** under the Christian Fiction genre. Her books include the Eugeena Patterson Mysteries, Joss Miller Mysteries, Serena Manchester Mysteries, Reed Family Mysteries, and the Victory Gospel Mysteries.

When Tyora isn't working for a literary client, she's either loving on her cats, listening to an audiobook or podcast, binge-watching crime shows or Marvel movies, and of course, thinking about the next book. To contact

Tyora about reviewing her books or book club discussions, visit her online at TyoraMoody.com.

Also By Tyora Moody

Eugeena Patterson Mysteries

Deep Fried Trouble, #1

Oven Baked Secrets, #2

Lemon Filled Disaster, #3

A Simmering Dilemma, #4

An Unsavory Mess, #5

A Spicy Predicament, #6

Eugeena Patterson Family Shorts

Shattered Dreams, #1

A Blended Family Christmas, #2

Falling in Love... Again!, #3

Joss Miller Mysteries

Double Mocha Blues, #1

Serena Manchester Mysteries

Hostile Eyewitness, prequel

Bittersweet Motives, #1

Dangerous Confessions, #2

Waning Innocence, #3

Presumed Guilty, #4

Reed Family Mysteries

Broken Heart, #1

Troubled Heart, #2

Relentless Heart, #3

With All My Heart, #3.5

Faithful Heart, #4

Wounded Heart, #5

Victory Gospel Series (Mysteries)

When Rain Falls, #1

When Memories Fade, #2

When Perfection Fails, #3

Victory Gospel Shorts (Sweet Romance)

The Replacement Date, #1

Southern Delights, #2

When Love Finds Me, #3

Nobody's Replacement, #4

A Southern Delights Christmas, #5

Holding on to Love, #6

www.ingramcontent.com/pod-product-compliance
Lightning Source LLC
LaVergne TN
LVHW010839120826
845149LV00017B/3307

* 9 7 8 1 9 6 1 4 3 7 1 6 6 *